Milky Way Railroad

KENJI MIYAZAWA

Milky Way Railroad

Translated and adapted from the Japanese by
Joseph Sigrist and D. M. Stroud

Illustrated by Ryu Okazaki

STONE BRIDGE FICTION
Stone Bridge Press
Berkeley, California

Published by
Stone Bridge Press, Inc., P.O. Box 8208, Berkeley, CA 94707
TEL 510-524-8732 • sbp@stonebridge.com • www.stonebridge.com

Original Japanese text begun in 1927, published
posthumously as *Ginga Tetsudo no Yoru.*

Excerpts from this translation were previously published
by *Japan Quarterly*, Tokyo, in 1984.

First Stone Bridge Fiction edition published 2008.

Cover design by Linda Ronan.

Text design inspired by D. M. Stroud and Brenda Cossé.

Printed in the United States of America.

ISBN 978-1-933330-40-2

Contents

Introduction

KENJI MIYAZAWA (1896–1933) WAS JAPAN'S BEST-LOVED CHILDREN'S
writer and one of its three greatest modern poets. He spent most
of his brief life in the cold, isolated prefecture of Iwate, hundreds
of miles north of Tokyo. Although he was well known in literary
circles and published in Tokyo magazines, Miyazawa devoted
most of his life to teaching school, when he was not engaged as
a chemist and government agricultural agent. To while away the
long winters, he created stunningly original poems and a series
of beautiful tales for children, one of which is translated here.

Miyazawa was well informed about most aspects of modern science, yet he devoted many years roaming from temple to

temple in search of the Buddhist doctrine that would best accommodate his syncretic religious beliefs. His fascination with Christianity led him to imagine a kind of universal dogma that would fuse Christianity and Buddhism. He seems to have been particularly taken with the relationship between Esoteric Buddhism and the Hermetic doctrines of Giordano Bruno and Tommaso Campanella, which attempted to reconcile Christianity and Renaissance science with alchemy, astrology, and Eastern esotericism. Bruno and Campanella, in turn, were closely associated with the scientific ideas of Galileo, another great hero of Miyazawa's.

Milky Way Railroad, probably written in 1927, is a masterpiece of transcendental realism, a children's science fiction fantasy that expresses in symbolic form many of Miyazawa's religious and personal beliefs. Its physical setting is the small riverside town of Hanamaki, on the banks of the Kitakami River, where Miyazawa spent most of his life. Hanamaki at that time was connected to the town of Kamaishi by a narrow-gauge railroad, the Iwate Line; the four stations on the galactic railroad in the story correspond to the four actual stops between Hanamaki and Kamaishi.

The time of year is Tanabata, the seventh night of the seventh month, celebrated by the old lunar calendar in August so that it coincides with Obon, the festival of dead souls. The Tanabata Festival was brought to Japan from China in the eighth century. It commemorates the love of two personified stars, both prominent in the summer sky: the Weaver (Vega, in the constellation Lyra, "Harp") and the Cowherd (Altair, in Aquila, "Eagle"). The Weaver was a princess who wove the garments of the gods. She lived on the east side of the Milky Way and became so devoted to her husband, the Cowherd, who lived to the west, that she began to neglect her weaving. Her father, the Master of Heaven, condemned the couple to be separated, but he allowed them to meet on one night a year, the night of the Milky Way Festival. According to one version of the story, if the princess's weaving during the year was satisfactory a boatman would come to ferry her across the Milky Way, but in years when her father was displeased he would cause it to rain, making passage by boat impossible. A flock of magpies would then spread their wings to create a bridge across the river. In some parts of Japan, as in Kenji's town, during the celebration of Tanabata and Obon small gourds are hollowed out, filled with lighted candles, and set adrift on the rivers to symbolize the boat as well as the soul's passage to heaven.

The two separated "lovers" in Miyazawa's story are both male. They are two friends and schoolmates, the poverty-stricken Giovanni, whose father, a fisherman, is miles away in Hokkaido, and Campanella, whose father is a professor. On the night of the festival, Campanella, against his will, joins the other boys in their mockery of Giovanni, and Giovanni goes off alone to mope at the top of a hill, where he is suddenly transported on a magical train to the Milky Way. While his friends are celebrating the yearly meeting of the Cowherd and the Weaver, Giovanni will be right up there with the stars. And better yet, he'll find his friend Campanella on the train with him.

Little does he realize, however, that Campanella has already drowned in the river below and that the train he is on is the train of death. Giovanni is the only one alive and the only one who will return to earth. But for this one night, he is alone with his best friend and nobody will interrupt their reverie. Perhaps Miyazawa was recalling a lost friend of his own or the recent death of his sister, or was describing the relation of the soul and its animus.

It is certain, however, that this story is a kind of Quest. The hero crosses the bridge of dreams after watching his friends sail the lighted gourds representing dead souls on the river below. Then, after climbing a magic mountain, he is given a ticket that takes him to a second river, the Silver River (as the Milky Way is called in Japanese). There he meets the dead souls themselves and visits Heaven. Later he returns over the same bridge and sees the heavenly river reflected in the river below.

This bridge fits nicely into the Japanese literary tradition, for the "Bridge of Dreams" (Yume no Ukihashi) is the title of the last book of the eleventh-century classic *The Tale of Genji*. But *Milky Way Railroad* is really a compendium of Eastern and Western myth and folklore. Here we have the scholar who sees the universe in a grain of sand, the bird catcher who is a dead ringer for Mozart's Papageno, the fields of light, the leaping dolphins (a key Hermetic image that, besides being a symbol of Apollo and the oracle at Delphi, is one of the eight auspicious signs of Mikkyo—Tantric Buddhism—and the derivation of one of the three sacred symbols of imperial rule in Japan, the *magatama*), the flocks of magpies who form the bridge that unites the Weaver and the Cowherd, the Northern and Southern Crosses, and the golden apples of the Hesperides. Miyazawa's own original mythmaking is at work in his depictions of the observatory, the lighthouse keeper, and the Pliocene beach.

More than the synthesis of East and West, it is Miyazawa's attempt to create a literature that fuses the imagery of religion and science that most sets him apart from other writers of his era. Many of his poems are nearly untranslatable, so clotted are they with these fusions of religious and scientific language. But in the purer, simpler vocabulary of *Milky Way Railroad*, the syncretism is more successful. Indeed, Miyazawa's playful conceptualizing often seems to anticipate later scientific discoveries. The multiple-mirror telescope in his observatory was not actually built until 1977. Likewise, his galactic Coal Sack suggests a knowledge of black holes that did not emerge until much later, and his speculation about powerful magnetic fields in the Milky Way was replicated by research at the National Science Foundation in 1986.

A devout Buddhist, Miyazawa was often used by the

wartime Japanese regime as a posthumous spokesman for their Shinto-based *yamato damashi* or "persistence in the face of the unbearable." Miyazawa, however, was delivering a strong message to children in favor of universal brotherhood and compassion. And it is significant for Japanese readers that he began this story in 1927, the year of Ryonosuke Akutagawa's tragic suicide. Akutagawa, a great writer who was dismayed with the militaristic trends of that time, died with an open Bible by his side and used in his suicide note the words *bonyari shita fuan* (a vague feeling of uneasiness), which Miyazawa repeats several times in the context of Giovanni's quest. The same note also contains a reference to the Milky Way.

Yet Miyazawa speaks not just the language of the stars, but also the language of everyday human discourse. And it is the marvelously constructed paradoxes of this tale that lift *Milky Way Railroad* beyond the level of ordinary children's literature. Giovanni is sent on an errand to bring milk to his mother, but can't do it until he returns from the Milky Way. The cow is out of milk just like the one in "Jack and the Beanstalk." Jack must find his way out of maternal dependence by climbing to heaven, just as Giovanni does as soon as he finds the Pillar of Heaven. This Pillar of Heaven is a reference to the "August Heavenly Pillar" of Japanese mythology, which Izanagi and Izanami must walk around before allowing their Moses-like son to float away in a reed boat.

His best friend, Campanella—representing the Weaver Maiden in the Tanabata legend—falls into the river in which the Milky Way is reflected. Giovanni must go to the Milky Way to find Campanella, but he also finds himself and learns some of the most important lessons of life from examples like the Scorpion, who is transformed into a constellation so he can serve others. Finally, Giovanni, the fatherless boy who yearns for his father's return, can't be reunited with his own father until his father's best friend, the professor, loses a son (Giovanni's own best friend).

One life ends, another begins. Giovanni has sampled both. As he turns from the gloomy bridge over the Kitakami River, he sees the entire gleaming Milky Way reflected in its waters, the river of earth joined to the river of sky in a perfect bond.

Just as he gave Japanese names to the obviously Western and Christian children on the train, Miyazawa gave his Japanese characters Italian names to emphasize the story's universality, even though it is set in the very rural part of Japan where he lived. The names are also a tribute to his hero, Tommaso Campanella (1568–1639). Campanella was originally christened "Giovanni," the name he used until he was fifteen. Thus the two boys, Campanella and Giovanni, are a kind of doppelganger, two aspects of the same child, one poor and reticent, the other rich and better educated. Campanella, who spent twenty-seven years in prison, part of them under torture in a lightless dungeon, wrote a utopian vision of a communist and sexually liberated world order in *La città del sole* (City of the Sun, 1602–23) and was an early champion of Galileo's scientific proofs that the earth revolved around the sun. He was arrested for leading an unsuccessful revolt against the Spanish conquerors of his native Calabria. Campanella, like Miyazawa, hoped to integrate modern science with both orthodox religion and the mystical concepts that pre-date both Buddhism and Christianity. There are very slight hints that Miyazawa also favored rebellion: Giovanni's father may be in jail because of a communist-inspired fishermen's revolt that was raging at that time in Hokkaido, the topic of a popular novel of the period, Takiji Kobayashi's *The Factory Ship* (1929).

Miyazawa, who was an avid opera fan and owned one of the largest record collections in his hometown, probably first became interested in this Italian rebel-philosopher through the 1828 opera *Masaniello* or *La Muette de Portici* by Auber and Scribe. One of the most popular operas of its day, whose most famous aria was frequently sung in concerts up to Miyazawa's time, it described another popular insurrection in the same part of Italy fifty years after Campanella. Miyazawa, in fact, was so impressed that he wrote a poem about Masaniello.

The name of a minor character, Zanelli, also suggests this link to opera and the fictional doubles of the story. Renato Zanelli (1892–1935) was one of the foremost operatic tenors and the most famous Othello of Miyazawa's day. He traveled and recorded widely, making twenty recordings for Victor in 1919, the year of his Metropolitan debut. Miyazawa would also have been fascinated with the fact that Zanelli switched in mid-career from baritone to tenor and had a brother, Carlo Morelli (1897–1970), who in true doppelganger fashion once appeared as Iago to his Othello in the Verdi opera.

This translation, originally completed by Joseph Sigrist in 1971, was substantially revised by me. It was first published in abridged form by *Japan Quarterly* in 1984 and subsequently was revised again.

D. M. STROUD

Afternoon Class

"WELL THEN, EVERYBODY, WHILE IT'S BEEN CALLED A
river or a leftover spill of milk, can you tell me if this
pale white thing is in fact a river?" The teacher pointed to the whitish Milky Way zone stretching from
top to bottom of the star map that hung over the
blackboard.

Campanella raised his hand. Four or five other
students raised theirs. Giovanni started to raise his
hand too, but quickly pulled it back. He felt sure
that he'd read once in a magazine that the Milky

Way was made up of stars, but recently he'd been in a continual daze, even in the classroom, and had neither free time to read books, nor books to read. He'd begun to feel that he didn't understand anything for certain.

But the teacher, only too quickly, noticed. "Giovanni, you must know."

Giovanni sprang to his feet, but found he had nothing to say. Zanelli squirmed around in the seat in front of him, looked back at Giovanni, and giggled. Giovanni turned beet red.

"If you examined the Milky Way with a large telescope, what would you find?"

They must be stars, thought Giovanni, but again he couldn't come out with the answer.

The teacher looked frustrated for a moment, but then turned to Campanella. "Well, then, Campanella!" And Campanella, who had only just then raised his hand so promptly, got up only with hesitation, having nothing in fact to say.

The teacher looked intently and with some

surprise at Campanella, but finally said, "Well then, that's enough," and pointed to the star map again himself. "If you looked at the pale white Milky Way through a powerful telescope, it would appear as a great number of little stars. Right, Giovanni?"

Giovanni, turning crimson, nodded, but at the same time his eyes brimmed over with tears. "But I knew!" he thought—and so, of course, did Campanella. It had been written up in a magazine he and Campanella had read, together at Campanella's house. (Campanella's father had a Ph.D.) Campanella had jumped up and brought a big book from his father's study, and, opening it at the place marked "Milky Way," the two of them had pored over a beautiful full-page photograph, completely black except for the little white points that covered it. "Campanella could hardly have forgotten something like that," thought Giovanni. "If he didn't answer, it must mean that he's thinking how hard I have to work morning and night. I've given up playing with the others when I come to school, or even talking

"SO THEN," THE TEACHER WAS SAYING, "IF WE THINK
THAT THIS HEAVENLY RIVER IS REALLY A RIVER,
ALL OF THOSE LITTLE STARS ARE LIKE THE SAND
AND GRAVEL IN THE RIVERBED."

much to Campanella. So, when he didn't answer on purpose, he must have been covering up for me." Giovanni felt an unbearable wave of sadness sweep over him, both for himself and for Campanella.

"So then," the teacher was saying, "If we think that this heavenly river is really a river, all of those little stars are like the sand and gravel in the river-bed. Or, if we think of the Milky Way as a great flow of milk, then it resembles a heavenly river even more. The stars are specks floating in the milk like drops of oil. And if you ask what compares to the water or milk of the river, we answer, 'the speed of light,' 'the vacuum.' The sun and the earth are floating in it. In short, we are floating in the water of the Milky Way River. And if we look in all directions from where we are within this watery space, we see the bluish tint of deep water. Now, down at the bottom, deep and far away, the stars are thickly concentrated, and so seem white to us. Look at this model."

The teacher pointed to a large, two-faced convex lens containing many shining grains of sand.

"The galaxy is shaped like this. Each of these bright pebbles, like our sun, is a shining star. Our sun is just about in the middle, and our earth is nearby. At night, you, who are standing, let us say, in the center of the lens, should take a look around. This part of the lens is thin so you can see only a few shining pebbles or stars. Over here and here, the glass is thick and the pebbles—the stars—are numerous. The faraway ones look white to us.

"Well then, so much for today's discussion of that great heavenly river, the Milky Way. The next questions, about how big the lens is and about the various stars within, will be our next science lesson, I guess. For now, time's up. Today is the Milky Way Festival, so all of you go outside and look at the sky tonight. That's all. Close your books and notebooks."

And for a moment the room was full of the sound of desks opening and closing, and of books piling up. Then everyone stood to attention and left the classroom.

The Print Shop

AS HE WENT OUT THE SCHOOLHOUSE GATE, GIOVANNI found seven or eight of his classmates who, instead of going home, had gathered around Campanella by the cherry tree in the corner of the school garden. They seemed to be talking about going to get the gourds which, hollowed out and fitted with candles, would be sailed down the river as part of tonight's Milky Way Festival.

But Giovanni, with a broad wave of his hand, hurried by and went on out the school gate. Each house he passed in the town had made various preparations for the festival—wreaths of yew leaves were hung out, and the branches of the cypress trees were strung with lights. Giovanni did not go straight home. Instead, he turned three corners and, removing his shoes, went into a spacious room where, although it was still day, the lights were on and a great number of rotary presses were churning and clanging away. Men with bands of cloth and eyeshades fitted around their heads were hard at work reading and counting in singsong voices.

Giovanni went straight to the man sitting at the third table from the front and bowed respectfully. "That's all we can pick up, is it?" said the man, after searching the shelves of type for awhile. He pushed a page of manuscript over to Giovanni. Taking a small flat box from under the table, Giovanni went over to the brightly lit area where racks of type were lined against the wall and began to pluck out the required bits of grainlike type, one by one, with a small pair of tweezers.

THE PLACE WHERE GIOVANNI WAS RUSHING SO EAGERLY
WAS A LITTLE HOUSE ON A SIDE STREET.

"Hey, Bug-eyes! How're you doing?" called a man wearing a blue vest as he passed behind Giovanni. Four or five men working nearby laughed mockingly, but did not turn around. Giovanni had to wipe his eyes often as he laboriously picked out the type, and finally, a little after six o'clock, he took the flat box, now full of the type he had compared with the manuscript, and brought it back to the man at the table. The man took the box without speaking and nodded slightly.

Giovanni bowed as he went out through the door and stopped at the accountant's desk. There a man dressed in white silently handed over a small silver coin to him. Giovanni's face suddenly brightened and, in high spirits, he took his bag of schoolbooks from the place where he had left it and went running out of the print shop. Whistling vigorously, he stopped at the bakery to buy a loaf of bread and a bag of sugar cubes before racing on at full speed.

Home

THE PLACE WHERE GIOVANNI WAS RUSHING SO EAGER-
ly was a little house on a side street. There, in the far-
thest left of three doorways, asparagus and purple kale
grew in an open box. The shades were pulled down
over two small windows. "Mother, I'm back! Are you
feeling all right?" Giovanni called out, as he slipped
out of his shoes.

When Giovanni came in, he found his mother
resting in the front room with a white cloth wrapped
around her head. "Ah—Giovanni, you must have

had a rough day. I've been feeling just fine. It was nice and cool today."

Giovanni opened a window. "Mom, I bought a bag of sugar today. I thought you'd like some sugar in your milk."

"Well, you have some first, Giovanni. I'm not hungry yet."

"Mom, when did Sis get back?"

"Ah, it was about three. She did all the house-work for me."

"Didn't your milk come, Mom?"

"It looks like it didn't."

"I'll go get it!"

"No, you go ahead and eat now. I can take my time later. Your sister made some kind of tomato dish and put it over there."

"Okay. I'll eat right away." Giovanni took the plate of tomatoes from the windowsill and sat for a while munching tomatoes and bread. "Oh. Mom," he broke out suddenly, "I'm quite sure Dad will be coming back before long!"

"I think so, too, but why do you think so, Giovanni?"

"It said in the paper this morning that the fishing was very good this year in the north."

"Ummm. But your father probably didn't go out to fish."

"Sure he did!" And Giovanni added, "He wouldn't do anything bad enough to be sent to jail. Remember the big crab shell and the reindeer antlers he gave to the school? Now they're in the display room, and the teachers take turns showing them in their classes."

"He said he'd bring you an otter-skin coat next time," said his mother.

"When the guys meet me, they all talk about that, too, to make fun of me."

"They make fun of you?"

"Yes, but Campanella never joins in. When they make remarks, Campanella just gets sort of sad-looking."

"Campanella's father and your father were

GIOVANNI TOOK THE PLATE OF TOMATOES FROM THE
WINDOWSILL AND SAT FOR A WHILE MUNCHING
TOMATOES AND BREAD.

friends when they were boys, just like you and Campanella are."

"That's why Dad took me with him to Campanella's house. Those were good times! I used to stop at Campanella's all the time on the way from school. There was a model train at Campanella's that ran with an alcohol engine. If you put together seven pieces of rail, they made a circle, and there were telephone poles and signal lights that turned green when the train was coming! Once when there wasn't any alcohol we used kerosene and the canister got covered with soot."

"Sounds logical," said Giovanni's mother.

"Now I go by there every morning on my paper route, but the house is always quiet and dark."

"Because it's so early."

"They have a dog called Pooch. His tail is just like a broom! When I go, he runs along beside me whining. He goes all the way to the corner in town with me. Sometimes even farther. Tonight," he went on, "everyone is going to sail gourds with candles down the river. I'm sure they'll take the dog."

"That's right, tonight's the Milky Way Festival, isn't it?"

"Yes. When I go for the milk, I'll go take a look."

"Yes, go right ahead!" urged his mother. "Only stay out of the river."

"I'll just be looking down from the rocks, and I'll be back in an hour."

"Play as much as you like. If you're with Campanella, I'm not worried."

"We'll be right together! Shall I close the window, Mom?"

"I guess so. It is getting cool."

Giovanni got up and closed the window. Then he washed the dishes, put away the bag of sugar and the bread, and, in high spirits, started out.

"I'll be back in an hour and a half, then," he called, and went out through the dark doorway.

The Milky Way
Festival

WITH A SAD FACE, GIOVANNI TRIED TO WHISTLE, BUT nothing would come out. He walked downhill on the road into town. It was lined with pitch black cypress trees. At the bottom of the slope a single lamppost shed a pale light. As Giovanni approached the light, his shadow, which up to then had trailed behind him—oblong, vague, and goblinlike—became steadily blacker and more distinct. Finally, with raised foot and waving hand, it came up alongside him. "I'm a locomotive now!" thought Giovanni to himself. "I'm speeding down this hill! Now I'm passing the street lamp and—hey!—now my shadow is a compass swinging around in front of me." As he crossed back and forth with long strides under the street lamp, his classmate Zanelli, wearing a new shirt with a long pointed collar, suddenly came out of a dark side street and hurried past Giovanni.

"Zanelli! Going to sail gourds?"

Before Giovanni could finish, the other boy snapped back over his shoulder, "Hey, Giovanni! Pop's sending an otter coat!"

Giovanni suddenly went cold and shaky inside. "What's that, Zanelli?" he shouted back shrilly, but Zanelli had already disappeared into a house with big cypress trees across the way. "Why does Zanelli say things like that when I haven't done anything to him?" wondered Giovanni. "And he's the one that looks like a rat when he runs. I guess he must be stupid if he says things like that to someone who hasn't done anything to him."

As these thoughts raced through Giovanni's

mind, he passed through the streets of the town, streets now festive indeed with their multitude of lights and long wreaths. Giovanni halted before the window of a watch repair shop which was illuminated with brilliant neon light. Second by second, the red eyes of a stone owl spun round and round, and the thick glass, the color of the sea, was radiant with jewel-like shimmerings. Slowly, like the stars, they revolved. And on the other side, a copper centaur turned gravely and slowly toward Giovanni. In the center was a round, black chart of the Milky Way decorated with green asparagus leaves.

Forgetful of all else, Giovanni stared in fascination at the star map. It was much smaller than the chart he'd seen at school. And it was made so that, if one turned its dial to match the day and hour, the appropriate configuration of the heavens would spin into view within the oval. The Milky Way stretched across the middle like a smoky sash, and the lower part seemed to rise like exploding steam. Behind the chart, a small golden telescope gleamed on its tripod, and at the back of the display hung a map of the constellations in the forms of fabulous beasts, snakes, and turtles. Was the sky, then, thickly packed with these figures of heroes and scorpions? "Ah," thought Giovanni, "how I'd like to walk through the sky and see." And he stood there gazing raptly for some time.

Then, suddenly remembering the milk for his mother, he left the store window. He strode on through town, swinging his arms and throwing out his chest, even though it made the coat pinch his shoulders.

The air had turned clear and flowed just like water through the streets and shops. The street lights were all decorated with pale branches of fir and oak, and the six trees in front of the electric company were strung with tiny electric lights. The whole town seemed like a city of mermaids.

The children in their newly pressed clothes went along whistling as if on their way to the stars. "Sagittarius, send down rain!" they shouted as they

THE RED EYES OF A STONE OWL SPUN ROUND AND
ROUND. . . . IN THE CENTER WAS A ROUND, BLACK
CHART OF THE MILKY WAY.

ran, gleefully setting off blue magnesium flares behind them. But Giovanni realized he couldn't join in the merrymaking, and, head down, he hurried on to get the milk. After a while he came to a place at the edge of town where row on row of tall poplar trees floated high in the starry sky. There he entered the darkened doorway of the dairy and stopped in front of the kitchen, which was gloomy and smelled of cows. Giovanni took off his hat.

"Good evening," he called. But the house was silent throughout, and there didn't seem to be anyone home. "Good evening! Anyone home?" he called again, drawing himself up to his full height. Finally an old woman, who looked rather sickly, came slowly out and muttered something unintelligible.

"The milk wasn't delivered to our home today, so I came by to pick it up," said Giovanni, emphasizing each word distinctly in case she was hard of hearing.

"There's no one here now, and I don't know anything about it, so come back tomorrow." The old woman rubbed a red spot under her eye and looked down at Giovanni.

"My mother's sick, so I really have to have the milk tonight."

"Well, then, come back a little later." So saying, the old woman turned away.

"Oh, well—thank you!" And Giovanni went out to the street again.

He no sooner reached the street corner when he saw six or seven tousled boys in rumpled shirts. Whistling and laughing, each one held a hollow gourd with a candle in it. As they came up to the general store across from him, Giovanni recognized them by their whistles and laughs. They were Giovanni's classmates. His heart thumping, he started to turn back. But then, thinking better of it, he kept on walking toward them.

"Going to the river?" Giovanni started to say with, he thought, a catch in his throat, when . . .

"Here comes the otter coat, Giovanni!" First

"I DON'T HAVE ANYWHERE TO PLAY AND BE HAPPY," HE WAS
THINKING, "AND THE OTHERS TREAT ME LIKE AN ANIMAL."

Zanelli shouted. Then they all joined in. "The otter coat's on the way, Giovanni!" they shouted over and over.

Giovanni flushed crimson and, no longer knowing whether he was walking or not, rushed blindly past. Then he noticed Campanella was with them. Campanella was silent and, with a slight, rather pained smile on his face, looked at Giovanni as if to say, "You won't be angry, will you?"

Giovanni avoided his glance and hurried by. They all began to whistle behind his back and then, as Giovanni looked behind at the next corner, he saw that Zanelli had turned around. Campanella, whistling loudly, was walking off toward the dim and distant bridge down at the river.

Giovanni felt a loneliness beyond words, and suddenly began to run. A crowd of little children, hopping along and shouting with their hands to their ears, stared after the running boy and shouted all the louder. Giovanni ran quickly on, but just as he started up the slope toward home, he veered away and headed instead toward the north edge of town. "I don't have anywhere to play and be happy," he was thinking, "and the others treat me like an animal."

On the bridge he stopped to catch his breath and whistled a little sigh of relief. He felt like crying but knew he shouldn't. After a brief rest, he went running on again, as fast as he could, into the dark shadow of the hill beyond.

The Pillar of Heaven

THE HILL ROSE IN BACK OF A FARM TO A POINT directly under the Big Dipper. Giovanni pressed on up a path through the woods, the grass beneath his feet wet with dew. The thin line of the path, glowing in the starlight, passed through black grass and dark thickets and bushes. In the grass fireflies twinkled, and their blue gleams, coming through the leaves, Giovanni took for the lights the boys had put in the gourds.

Going beyond the pitch black pines and oaks, he came suddenly into a clearing, and as the sky opened out above him, he saw the brilliant white Milky Way stretching from south to north. A pole marked the hill's summit under mid-heaven. Wildflowers carpeted the ground, exhaling a dreamlike fragrance. Over the hilltop a single bird passed, warbling.

Giovanni threw his heaving body down on the cold grass by the pole. The lights of the town shone up from below like the view of some shrine on the ocean floor. Very faintly he could hear the whistling and singing of the children, and occasionally a faraway cry. There was the distant rushing of the wind, and the quiet rustling of the grass around him. Giovanni's sweat-soaked shirt grew cool.

Across the fields came the sound of a train. The line of windows in the coaches looked small and red. Inside, the passengers must be laughing and eating apples and doing all sorts of things. And Giovanni, again feeling a deep sadness, looked toward the sky.

However he looked at it, he couldn't think of the sky as the cold, vacant place the teacher talked about at school. Somewhere up there—one could

44

AS THE SKY OPENED OUT ABOVE HIM, HE SAW THE BRILLIANT
WHITE MILKY WAY STRETCHING FROM SOUTH TO NORTH.

almost see them! There must be little woods and farms and fields. Giovanni looked at the stars around Vega. There were three or four of them in a clump, twinkling and winking down. Now they extended a beam of light like an outstretched leg, now they pulled it back. Now that clump of stars was like a mushroom resting on a starbeam stem.

In fact, all those twinkling stars gathered together, stretching to the town at his feet, looked like one great cloud of smoke.

Milky Way Station

AND THEN GIOVANNI FOUND THAT THE POLE BEHIND him had become a triangular signpost. For some moments it flickered off and on like a lightning bug and then, brighter and sharper, it became a fixed beacon. The sign stood in the dark, steel blue sky like a newly forged steel post planted straight and firm in the celestial fields.

Giovanni heard a strange voice calling, "Milky Way Station! Milky Way Station!" All at once everything before his eyes was illuminated, as if a billion fireflies had been fixed in one perpetual flash and inlaid in the sky. Or as if all the world's diamonds, that the diamond companies hide in order to keep prices up, had been abruptly dumped out and scattered recklessly all over.

As everything suddenly brightened, Giovanni couldn't help rubbing his eyes again and again. Then, looking intently around, Giovanni discovered he was in a small railroad coach which was clickety-clacking along a narrow track. He was, in fact, riding the night train on a narrow-gauge line in a small, yellow, brightly lit coach, and he was looking out the window. The inside of the coach seemed perfectly empty. The seat covers were made of green velvet, and the wall across from him was polished with gray varnish and adorned with two big brass studs. Then Giovanni noticed that, in the seat right in front of him, a tall boy in a wet-looking overcoat was sticking his head out the window and looking outside. "Those shoulders certainly look familiar," thought

Giovanni, and he was seized by an irresistible desire to find out who it was.

As Giovanni started to put his head out the window, the other boy pulled his own back in and looked around at Giovanni.

It was Campanella! Giovanni was going to say, "Campanella, you were here all along!" but before he could say anything, Campanella spoke. "They were all running, too, but they couldn't keep up. Zanelli, too. He ran fast, but he couldn't catch up."

Giovanni thought, "That's how it was . . . we went off together," and he said, "Shall we wait for him somewhere?"

"Zanelli went home. His father came to get him."

And, for some reason, Campanella's face turned a bit pale as he spoke then, as if something were hurting him inside. Then Giovanni, too, feeling as if he'd forgotten something somewhere, felt funny, and lapsed into silence. Campanella peered out the window. "Darn! I forgot to bring my canteen. And I forgot my sketchbook, too! But who cares! We'll be at the Swan Stop soon, and if we'll be looking at swans, I like that. Say—we're way past the river—that's for sure!"

Campanella was turning around a map made like a round board and looking at it from all angles. And there on that curious map was the Milky Way marked all in white and, along its left side, a single railway track tracing its way to the south.

The fine thing about the map was that on its surface, black as night, all of the railroad stations, signals, ponds, and forests were engraved in blue, orange, and green.

"Where did you get this map?"asked Giovanni. "It's made of obsidian."

"They gave it to me at Milky Way Station. Didn't you get one, too?"

"Oh, so we've passed Milky Way Station? That means we must be about here then." Giovanni found a point just north of the place where "Swan" was written.

"Right. Hey, is that moonlight on the riverbed?" And they saw that on the shimmering edge of the Milky Way, heavenly fields of marsh grass were glistening silver and murmuring wavelike in the wind.

"That's not moonlight—it's the light of the Milky Way," said Giovanni, and, scraping his feet as he swung from the window's edge, he put his head out of the train and whistled shrilly into the stars. Stretching as far as he could, he tried to see if there was any water in that heavenly river, but, at first, no matter how hard he tried he couldn't make it out clearly. But gradually, as he looked more intently, that clear water—more transparent than glass, or even hydrogen—broke into tiny purple waves (or was it his eyes?) and, sparkling like a rainbow, flowed soundlessly on. Here and there in the field stood phosphorescent reflecting signals. The distant ones were small, the nearby ones larger. The far-off signs were bright orange or yellow and clearly visible, while the closer signs were a shimmering blue or white. The signals, triangular or square or zigzag like lightning, or formed like chains, aligned in various ways, filled the entire field with light.

Giovanni, his heart beating fast, tossed his head wildly. And that entire field of blues and oranges, the many radiant signposts, pulsated as though they were breathing in and out. "I'm really up in the sky," said Giovanni. And, now sticking out his left hand and looking toward the front of the train, he went on, "This train isn't burning coal, is it?"

"It probably runs on alcohol or electricity," said Campanella.

Then, just as if in answer to their question, from a misty great distance came a booming cellolike voice, "This train runs on neither steam nor electricity. It runs simply because it is so willed. And you think that it is making noise only because until now you have always ridden in trains that made noise."

"That voice! I've heard it often before . . . somewhere . . ."

"Me, too. It was in the woods, or by the river."

With a steady chug-chug, the little train went

THE YELLOW CUPS OF COUNTLESS GENTIANS GUSHING COLOR
LIKE RAIN FLOWED BEFORE THEIR EYES, AND THE LINE OF
SIGNALS STOOD BLINKING THEIR LIGHTS LIKE SMOKE, LIKE FIRE.

on through the fields of heavenly marsh grass waving in the breeze, on through the faint blue light of the triangular signals, on by the water of the great river, on and on it went.

"Oh! Gentian flowers. It's fall, then, for sure!" cried Campanella, pointing out the window. There were gentians inlaid like moonstones in the short grass along the track.

"I'm going to jump out and pick some, and then get back on board," said Giovanni excitedly.

"Too late—they're way behind us now," replied Campanella, but while he said this they came up to, and passed, another bed of gentians. And the yellow cups of countless gentians gushing color like rain flowed before their eyes, and the line of signals stood blinking their lights like smoke, like fire.

Northern Cross
and Pliocene Seashore

"WILL MY MOTHER EVER FORGIVE ME?" SAID CAM-panella, with a bit of a stammer.

"Oh, my mother!" thought Giovanni. "She's way out there, maybe near one of those far-off orange signals that looks like a speck of dust, and she's thinking of me." And Giovanni sank into a silent reverie.

"I'd do anything to make my mother really happy," said Campanella. "But what would really make her happiest?" He seemed to be struggling to hold back tears.

"Is something bad wrong with your mother?" Giovanni cried out in shock.

"I don't know," Campanella replied, "but if you do something really good, that's the best present for a mother . . . so I guess she'll forgive me." And he seemed to have come to some kind of decision.

Suddenly the inside of the car burst into a white glow. A single island came into sight in the midst of the voiceless flow of the gorgeous Milky Way River. And that island cast a halo of white light as if all the splendor of diamonds and the gleaming of grass were concentrated in one place. On the island's flat summit stood, ah, so vividly, a white cross. Silently, it stood as though hewn out for eternity from the clouds of the frozen North Pole. And it, too, shed a halo of light.

"Alleluia! Alleluia!" Voices rose from all sides. Turning around, Giovanni saw that the passengers (there were quite a number now!) were standing stiffly at attention, some holding black Bibles to their breasts, others crystal prayer beads. All of them had their hands reverently clasped. Instinctively, the two boys also rose to their feet. Campanella's cheeks sparkled like bright red apples.

By and by, the island and the cross passed behind them. Across the way now were cliffs and palely colored smoke which, like the marsh grass drifting in the breeze, now and again veiled the cliffs in silver as if they were breathing. And how many gentians there were!—now peeping out of the grass, now lost to sight, like gentle will-o'-the-wisps. The space between the river and the train was screened by marsh grass. Twice they caught a glimpse of the Swan Island, but it quickly became small and distant like a picture, and then it vanished behind the rustling marsh grass. Behind Giovanni was a tall Catholic nun (Giovanni couldn't remember when she had gotten on) with a black wimple. Her eyes were lowered and directed straight before her, as if she were reverently listening for something, for some words or some voice.

As the passengers returned to their seats, Giovanni and Campanella began to talk more freely, though a new feeling, not unlike deep sadness, was in their hearts.

"We'll be at Swan Station soon."

"At eleven o'clock, right on schedule!"

Quickly the green lights of the signals and the white posts flashed past the window. The light of the automatic switch, like a sulfur flame, passed beneath, and the train, easing down, came within sight of the line of lampposts at the station. Those lights grew bigger, and spread out, and they found themselves coming to a stop right in front of Swan Station's big clock. On the fresh autumn face of the clock two cobalt blue hands were pointing exactly to eleven o'clock. Everyone got off at once, and the inside of the car was left empty. "Twenty Minute Rest Stop" was written under the clock.

"How about us getting out, too?" asked Giovanni.

"Let's go."

Jumping up, they dashed out of the train and on through the station. Beyond the ticket window was the purple light of a single street lamp, but no one was to be seen. Looking all around, they could see no trace of anyone—neither stationmaster, nor redcaps. And so they came out on a small crystal-like plaza lined with ginkgo trees. From the plaza a broad street ran straight into the heart of the Milky Way's blue light.

The other passengers from the train, wherever they had gone, were nowhere to be seen. The boys, squaring their shoulders, started down the white road. Their shadows, like the shadows of two posts in a room illuminated from all sides, spread out in all directions like the countless spokes of a wheel. Soon they came to the beautiful riverbed they had seen from the train. Campanella, taking a pinch of sand and rubbing it back and forth in the palm of his hand, said dreamily, "These grains of sand are all crystal. And there are little flames inside each one."

"That's right," Giovanni answered vaguely, thinking, "He must have learned that somewhere." The pebbles of the riverbed were all transparent. Some were crystal and others topaz, some were rough, uncut stones, and some—the jade stones—glimmered with pale, faceted light. Giovanni ran down to the water's edge and dipped his hand in the water—that curious water of the Milky Way River which was more transparent than hydrogen. But the boys could tell the water was flowing because their wrists seemed to be bathed in a faint mercury color, and the waves that struck them made beautiful phosphorescent flares which twinkled and blazed. Looking upstream, they saw, under a cliff overgrown with marsh grass, a white rock plateau as flat as a football field, extending along the river. Against the stone they could see the shadows of five or six men who, bending over, seemed to be either burying something or digging it up. From time to time, light glinted from their spades and shovels.

"Let's go take a look!" Giovanni and Campanella cried out together and set off running. At the foot of that rocky white plateau hung a porcelain signboard reading "Pliocene Seashore." By the waterside a steel railing was planted, and nicelooking wooden benches were set up.

"Huh! There's something funny here," said Campanella, stopping in his tracks in amazement and picking up a long, black, thick, pointed walnutlike object from the rocks below.

"It's a walnut—and there're lots of them! And they didn't float down the river since they're up in the rocks."

"It's pretty big for a walnut—about twice as big as usual. And it hasn't gone bad yet, not even a bit."

"Let's go over where they're digging."

And carrying the jagged black walnuts, they continued along the path. The waves lapped against the shore on their left like surges of gentle lightning, and the nodding crests of marsh grass on the cliff to their right looked like silver and seashells.

Coming closer, they saw a tall, scholarly look-

"IT'S PRETTY BIG FOR A WALNUT—ABOUT TWICE AS BIG AS
USUAL. AND IT HASN'T GONE BAD YET, NOT EVEN A BIT."

ing man wearing boots and thick concave spectacles who was busy taking down something in a notebook and giving terse orders to his three assistants. These men were working away with pickaxes and shovels. "Careful with your shovels—don't break that projection there! Hey, you there—dig a little farther over! No! No! That's no good! What are you digging so violently for?" And they saw that the great white bones of some huge beast, fallen over on its side, had been more than half excavated out of the smooth white rock. Looking closely, they saw that a rock with two hoofprints in it had been neatly cut out and labeled in ten square pieces.

"You boys sightseeing?" asked the professor as he looked their way, his glasses glinting. "I suppose you saw all the walnuts. Those walnuts are, let's see, about 1,200,000 years old. Still quite fresh, eh? Around here at the shore everything is from 1,200,000 years ago—the latter part of the Tertiary Period. And we get seashells, too. Out there where the current flows there's salt water, ebbing and flowing, you know. This beast, now, is called a Bossy. . . . Hey there! Yes, you! That's enough with the pickax! Do it gently, with a chisel!

"It's called a Bossy, I was saying, and it's the ancestor of the present-day cow. There were a lot of them back then, you can bet your boots!"

"Are you going to make specimens out of it?"

"No. We need it for evidence. Now we feel this is a rich, thick stratum which, as various things attest, was formed 1,200,000 years ago. But the fellows who look at it differently from us will want proof from this stratum, won't they now? Or they might say we were taken in by the effects of wind or water or empty sky, see what I mean? . . . Hey! Oh, no! Not with that shovel! Don't you know the ribs will be right under there?" The professor ran off excitedly.

"It's time. We'd better go," said Campanella, checking his map against his wristwatch.

"Please excuse us. We have to go now," Giovanni called out politely to the professor.

"Must you? Well, goodbye then." And the professor went back to supervise, pacing this way and that.

The two boys ran as fast as they could across the white boulders, hurrying so as not to miss their train. They found they could run like the wind without losing their breath or getting hot around the knees. "If I could keep going like this, I could run all around the world," thought Giovanni. They came to the broad avenue, and the lampposts at the ticket booth gradually grew larger. Before they knew it, they were sitting in their old seats in the train and looking out the window at the way they had come.

The Bird Catcher

"WOULD YOU MIND IF I SAT HERE?"

They heard a quavering but kindly adult voice behind them. It was a man with a red beard and bent back who was carrying two bundles wrapped in white cloth over his shoulders. He was wearing a brown and rather tattered topcoat.

"Sure, go ahead," answered Giovanni with a slight shrug of his shoulders.

The man chuckled faintly in his whiskers and slowly placed his bundles on the rack above them.

Giovanni, feeling once again very lonely and sad, was silently staring at the clock on the station wall when, far ahead, there came a shrill noise like a glass whistle, and the train began to glide forward. Campanella was letting his eyes wander across the ceiling of the car. A black beetle was resting on one of the lights, and its shadow, grown huge, loomed all across the ceiling. The red-bearded man, smiling at some memory of his own, looked fondly at Giovanni and Campanella. The train picked up speed and the marsh grass and the river shone, in their ever-changing pattern, through the window.

"Where are you two going?" the man with the red beard asked a bit timidly.

"We're going on to the end," Giovanni answered.

"That's good enough. Indeed, this train does go on to the end."

"And where are you going?" Campanella asked abruptly, in a hostile tone. Giovanni broke out laughing, and a man across from them, with a pointed hat and a large key hanging at his waist, turned toward them and also laughed. So finally Campanella, too, began to giggle in embarrassment.

But, a dimple creasing his cheek, the man answered without a hint of annoyance, "I'm getting off just up the line here. My job is catching birds."

"What kind of birds?"

"Cranes and wild geese. Snowy herons and swans."

"Are there many cranes?"

"That there are. They were calling a bit back there—didn't you hear them?"

"No."

"Why, I believe I can still hear them now. Prick up your ears and listen!"

The two boys raised their heads and strained their ears. From between the chugging of the train and the rustling of the wind in the marsh grass they heard a crying like the lapping of water.

"How do you catch cranes?"

"Are you asking about cranes or about snowy herons?"

"Snowy herons," Giovanni answered, thinking that it made no difference.

"That's right easy. The herons flock together like the sand of the galactic river, and I can catch them in a snap. And I'm always there, you know, down by the riverside waiting for them. The heron puts its feet down like this, coming in for a landing, and snatch! I have it then, just as it touches down. The herons flock together and die peacefully. Afterward, of course, I make pressed leaves out of 'em, and that's it."

"You make pressed leaves out of snowy herons? For specimens?"

"Not specimens. To eat, of course."

"That's funny." Campanella tilted his head to one side doubtfully.

"There's nothing funny or peculiar about it. Here, now!" He stood up and, taking one bundle from the rack, undid it with a nimble whirling of his fingers.

"Look at this! I just caught these now."

"It's really heron!" They both exclaimed in spite of themselves.

Ten heron bodies, glittering pure white like that Northern Cross, were lined up, somewhat flattened, their black legs pulled in as if in repose.

"Their eyes are shut." Campanella gently touched the herons' crescent-shaped eyes with his finger. The birds' heads were topped with spearlike tufts of feathers.

"Certainly they're shut," said the bird catcher, and, rearranging the package, he wrapped it up again and secured it with a string.

"Do snowy herons taste good?" asked Giovanni, wondering if there were people around here who ate strange stuff like that.

"Delicious! I get orders every day. But I sell more of the wild geese. The wild geese have more bulk, and they're no trouble at all to prepare. Look!" The bird catcher undid yet another packet. In it, wild geese, complete with bills, were lined up somewhat flattened, just like the herons had been. They were a dappled yellow and cream color and, somehow, glowed with a shimmering light. "You can eat these just as they are. How about it? Go ahead and try some," said the bird catcher, gently tugging off the yellow leg of a goose. And, as if it were made of chocolate, the leg came off neat and clean. "How about it? Try some." And the bird catcher divided it in two and passed it over. Giovanni took a bite. "Why, this is cake! It tastes better than chocolate," he thought. "But there can't be birds flying around that taste like this. This fellow must have a bakery in the field somewhere. But then it won't do to make fun of him at the same time I'm eating his cake."

"Have some more," said the bird catcher again, holding out the package.

"No, thank you," said Giovanni, although he really wanted to eat more.

The bird catcher offered some to the man with the key sitting across the aisle. "Oh, no. It won't do, eating your merchandise," said the gentleman, tipping his hat.

"Don't give it a thought. How are the migratory birds getting on this year?"

"Ah, now, that's a fine state of affairs. The day before yesterday—it was about the second watch—the telephone was flooded with complaints from all over. They wanted to know why the lighthouse beam had been blacking out. But, my goodness! It wasn't me who blacked out the light. Black clouds of migrating birds were crossing in front of the light, and what are we to do about that, I ask you? Idiots! Instead of bringing their fool complaints to me, they could find some official with a shabby coat and a silly face and ask him to file their complaint for them. And that's what I told them!"

The fields gleamed brightly, now that the screen of marsh grass was gone.

"Why are herons more bother than wild geese?" asked Campanella, who had wanted to ask that question for some time.

The bird catcher turned back toward them. "To eat the snowy heron, you must either hang it out for ten days in the light of the water of the Milky Way or bury it in the sand for three or four days.

Then, when the mercury has all evaporated, you can eat it."

"This is no bird! It's just like cake, isn't it?" Campanella ventured to ask, since the bird catcher seemed to be hinting at the same thing.

The bird catcher, however, became very flustered. "Yes . . . ah! I must get off here," and he stood up, retrieved his bundles, and disappeared, just like that.

"Where'd he go?" The boys exchanged surprised glances, but the lighthouse keeper only grinned and, craning his neck, peered past them out the window. And they looked out, too. There in the low grass on the right bank of the river was the bird catcher they had just been talking to. Only now he was staring up at the sky with his arms spread and a look of great concentration on his face. He was glowing with a pale yellow phosphorescence.

"How did he get out there? That's really strange. He must be out to catch birds again, but the birds better come before the train goes by."

At that very moment herons, like the ones they had seen before, came out of the empty violet sky. They came dancing down in a great cloud like falling snow, calling as they came. The bird catcher gleefully—as if this were just what he'd ordered—planted his legs at exactly a 60-degree angle and, one after another, grabbed the descending herons by their retracted black legs and stuffed them in a cloth bag. The herons inside the bag could be seen flashing on and off like fireflies. At last, the blue flashes subsiding, they turned a dull white and closed their eyes. But the birds that landed safely uncaptured on the sand of the Milky Way River were even more numerous than the birds that were taken. As the boys watched, no sooner did the herons touch the sand than, just like melting snow, they began to dissolve and flatten out. Quickly, like molten copper discharged from a blast furnace, they spread over the sand and pebbles, where they left bird-shaped imprints. The prints pulsed brightly two or three times, then faded into the sand. The bird catcher put twenty herons in his bag and then sud-

"THE HERON PUTS ITS FEET DOWN LIKE THIS, COMING IN
FOR A LANDING, AND SNATCH! I HAVE IT THEN."

denly threw up both hands like a soldier struck by a fatal bullet. And before they could look twice, the bird catcher was no longer there.

But . . . "Ah . . . that was so good! You see . . . the secret is only to do just the amount of work that feels right for you," came a familiar voice at Giovanni's side. Giovanni saw the bird catcher neatly arranging the herons he had taken and piling them one on top of the other.

"How did you come from there to here all at once?" asked Giovanni, feeling strongly suspended between the ordinary and the extraordinary.

"How you say? I came because I decided to. And, by the way, where in the world do you boys come from?"

Giovanni meant to answer right off, but, in fact, he couldn't think where in the world he had come from. And Campanella flushed, as if trying to remember.

"From far away, aren't you?" said the bird catcher, simply nodding to himself as if he understood.

Giovanni's Ticket

"NOW THIS IS THE END OF THE SWAN ZONE HERE. AND look over there—that's the famous Leo Observatory." Outside their window, in the middle of the fireworks of the Milky Way, stood four big black buildings with flat roofs. On one roof, two large transparent balls of sapphire and topaz were rotating quietly in a circle. As the yellow one slowly turned to the far side, the blue one came over to the front. Presently their edges appeared to overlap, forming a beautiful green double-edged convex lens. The middle of the lens swelling out, the blue globe passed directly in front of the yellow topaz, and there was a green center ringed by a bright yellow circle. Then the lens shape reappeared in reverse, and, abruptly coming apart, the sapphire went to the far side and the yellow globe came to the front, returning to their original positions.

The black observatory lay as if asleep, surrounded by the formless, soundless water of the Milky Way.

"It's a machine to measure the water speed. The water ... ," began the bird catcher.

"Tickets, please!" interrupted a tall, red-capped conductor who had just come up and was standing in the aisle beside their seats. The bird catcher silently drew a slip of paper from his pocket. The conductor gave it a glance and then, turning to the boys, extended his hand toward Giovanni with a finger wagging, as if to say, "How about you?"

"Uh," Giovanni fidgeted in embarrassment, but Campanella, as if there were nothing to it, produced a gray ticket. Giovanni, in complete confusion, reached his hand into his coat pocket, on the off chance that there might be something there, and his fingers encountered some kind of big folded paper. Wondering how it had gotten there he pulled it out and found it was a piece of green paper, about the size of a postcard, folded in four. The conductor's hand was still extended, so, thinking it would do no harm and he might as well try, Giovanni handed it over. The conductor drew himself up straight and, opening the paper, inspected it carefully. While he was reading, the conductor adjusted his coat buttons and the lighthouse keeper tried to steal a peek at the mysterious paper from below. Giovanni, thinking it must be a certificate of some kind, felt his heart pounding.

"Did you bring this from the Third Dimension?" asked the conductor.

"I don't know." Giovanni, relieved that everything seemed to be all right, chuckled nervously.

"It's quite in order. We will arrive at the Southern Cross at about the next third interval." The conductor, returning the paper to Giovanni, went on to the next seat.

Campanella at once peered impatiently at the paper to find out what it was, and Giovanni, too, was eager to see what was on it after all. There were just ten strange characters printed on the ticket against a pattern of black arabesques. As he stared silently at the pattern, Giovanni felt as though it were sucking him inside.

Just then the bird catcher, who had been standing alongside looking intently at the ticket, spoke out excitedly. "Say! This is really something! It's a ticket for going straight to outer space. Not for just one place or another, either. It's a free pass to space. You can go anywhere you please. In fact, with this ticket, you can go anywhere on this imperfect, fantasy Fourth Dimension Milky Way Railroad. You're really sitting pretty!"

"Well, doesn't that beat everything!" said Giovanni, flushing, and, refolding his ticket, he put it away in his pocket.

He gazed self-consciously out the window again with Campanella, but out of the corner of his eye he could see the bird catcher looking sideways at him, as if to say, "That's really something!"

"We'll be at Eagle Station any minute." Campanella was comparing his map with three small pale triangular signals standing on the bluff opposite them.

Giovanni now, without knowing why, began to feel a strange, unbearable sympathy for the man next to him. He thought of the bird catcher catching herons, and happily saying, "Ah, that was so good!" and wrapping the birds in white cloth, and looking sideways in amazement at Giovanni's ticket, and finally exclaiming in surprise at it. As he thought of these things one after another, he was seized with the desire to do something for this stranger of a bird catcher, to give him something to eat, or anything. If it would really make the bird catcher happy, Giovanni was ready to stand on the radiant bank of the Milky Way River catching birds himself, even for a hundred years. He thought to ask, "What is it that you really want?" But that seemed too forward. Wondering how to put it, he looked around. But the bird catcher had vanished.

The white bundles, too, were gone from the luggage rack. Quickly he looked outside, thinking he might see the bird catcher again looking up at the sky, his feet planted firmly on the ground, preparing to catch herons. But outside there was only the carpet of lovely pebbles and the waves of marsh grass. The broad back and peaked red cap of the bird catcher were nowhere to be seen.

"Where did he go?" asked Campanella, somewhat stunned.

"Where did he go?" echoed Giovanni. "I think we'll meet him again somewhere . . . there was something I had to say to him."

"Yes—me, too."

"I thought he was kind of a nuisance, so I guess I was rough on him." It was really the first time Giovanni had ever experienced this strange kind of feeling, and the first time he'd ever said anything like that, either, he thought.

Shipwrecked Children

"SOMETHING SMELLS LIKE APPLES OR MAYBE I WAS just thinking of apples." Campanella looked around in wonder.

"It's an apple smell, all right—that and wild roses, too." Giovanni looked all around and decided the scent must be coming from outside. "But," he thought, "it's fall now, so why should it smell like wild roses?"

And the next moment, a boy barely six years old, with shiny black hair, an unbuttoned red jacket, and a terribly startled look on his face, was standing there—shivering and barefoot. Next to him stood a tall clean-cut young man in a black suit. Poised like a tree standing against a strong wind, he held the boy's hand tightly.

"Oh, my! Where are we? It's so pretty!" Behind the young man stood a cute, brown-eyed girl in a black coat. She looked about twelve years old. Clutching the young man's arm, she stared out the window in amazement.

"This must be Lancashire—no, wait a minute—it's Connecticut. No—we're in the sky and we're going to Heaven. Look! That mark is the sign of Heaven. There's nothing to be afraid of now. We've been called to God." The black-suited young man beamed with joy as he spoke to the girl. But then for some reason he frowned deeply and, forcing a smile, as if in utter exhaustion, set the little boy down next to Giovanni and gently showed the girl to the seat next to Campanella.

The girl sat down obediently and neatly folded

her hands. But the boy was not so meek. "I want to go where my daddy and big sister are," he said to the young man, who now sat opposite the lighthouse keeper. The young man looked back wordlessly at the boy's damp, curly hair with a very sorrowful and intent expression. And the girl, suddenly covering her face with both hands, broke down in sniffles.

"Dad and sister Kikuyo still have some work to do, but they'll be here real soon," said the young man. "And think of how long your mother's been waiting. She's thinking 'What song is my sweet little Tadashi singing now?' or of you joining hands with the others that snowy morning, dancing around the bush in the garden. She's really waiting and worrying. So let's go see Mother as fast as we can, right?"

"Um . . . But I wish I hadn't gotten on that ship," said the little boy.

"Yes. But look around. See the sky! That beautiful river! Over there when you sang, 'Twinkle, twinkle, little star' all summer at bedtime you could look out the window and see the white Milky Way faintly gleaming in the distance. But this is it, see? It's beautiful, isn't it? Look how it shines!"

The boy's sister wiped her eyes with a handkerchief and looked out the window. The older boy said quietly and instructively, "There'll be no more sad things now. We're on our way through this nice place, and soon we'll be where God is. Where God is, there are all sorts of nice, happy, sweet people. And the people who got on the lifeboat instead of us will be safely on their way to their own homes and their worried mothers and fathers. So . . . we'll be arriving soon. Cheer up, and let's sing something lively as we go."

He stroked the wet black hair of the boy, and, as he comforted the others, his own face gradually brightened.

"Where did you people come from? What happened?" the lighthouse keeper asked, as if he'd only barely caught on.

The young man smiled faintly. "Oh . . . our ship hit an iceberg, and sank. Their father had been called back home in an emergency, about two months ago. And we started out a little later. I was going to college and working as the family's private tutor. Then on the twelfth day out—it was today or yesterday—the ship struck an iceberg and immediately keeled over and started to sink. There was faint moonlight in places, but the fog was very thick. And on top of that, half the boats on the port side were unusable, so it was clear that not everyone could be saved. So there was the ship about to go down any minute, and I got desperate and started shouting for them to get these children into the lifeboats. The people nearby made way and picked up the cry, pleading for the children. But the space in front of the lifeboats was crowded with children and parents, and I hardly had the heart to push my way through. But still I felt it was my duty to save these children by all means, so I tried to push them forward. Then, again, I thought, really the best thing for the children might be to go now, together, to be with God—better than to be saved this way. But if the

"I GOT DESPERATE AND STARTED SHOUTING
FOR THEM TO GET THESE CHILDREN INTO THE LIFEBOATS."

sin against God could be mine alone, I would try to save them by any means.

"But I couldn't do anything. As they pushed their children into the lifeboats and parted from them, the mothers tossed kisses wildly, while the fathers stood silently by, trying to hold back their emotions. It was heartbreaking. All the while, the ship was sinking rapidly, so we grouped together, and, ready for the worst, I embraced these two and waited for the ship to sink. I thought we should try to float in the water if we could. With all my strength, I pulled a wooden grating from the deck, and the three of us clung to it. Then someone began to sing a hymn (it was Number 306), and, in no time, everyone was singing together—each in his own language. Then there was a loud noise, and we were in the water. We got caught in a whirl-pool, and I held on to these children as tight as I could—but then everything went blank, and the next thing I knew we were here.

"Their mother had passed away a year ago. I'm

sure those boats got away safely. With skilled sea-men at the oars, they moved away from the ship in a hurry."

Imagining the sighs and pleas of the children on the ship, Giovanni and Campanella suddenly remembered long forgotten things and their eyes welled hot with tears.

"Maybe that great ocean is the Pacific," thought Giovanni. "The far north of that ocean, where ice-bergs flow. There are people in small boats. Buffet-ed by wind and icy water, they are beating back the violent cold. I'm sorry for those people, and I feel wrong about not helping them. But what on earth can I do for their happiness?" Giovanni, completely downcast, lowered his head.

Then the lighthouse keeper said reassuring-ly, "Who knows if it wasn't all for the best? Really, however bitter a thing is, if it finds you walking the right road, whether you're going up or down, either way you come step by step nearer to true happiness."

"That's true. And in order to reach true happiness, you have to suffer a lot," said the young man. At his side, the brother and sister both lay back exhausted in their seats, sound asleep. The boy's feet, which had been bare, now rested in soft white shoes.

The train chugged on along the bank of the lovely phosphorescent river, and the field visible through the windows opposite looked just like a slide from a magic lantern. Triangular signs—a hundred, no, a thousand of them, some big and some small—completely covered the end of the field and, on the larger ones, speckled red surveying flags were mounted. The countless signal lights from the tops of the hills made a fog of pale blue fire and, from there, or somewhere beyond, shapes like skyrockets drifted one after another into the violet sky. And the transparent wind was indeed charged with the scent of roses.

"You probably haven't had this kind of apple before. Why not try one?" The lighthouse keeper had a pile of big gleaming golden apples in his lap. Carefully he held them so as not to let any fall.

"Huh! Where did they come from? Do they

grow apples like this around here? They're beautiful!" the young man exclaimed with real surprise,
completely absorbed, his eyes wide and his neck
craned at the apples the lighthouse keeper held in
his hands.

The young man took one and glanced toward
Giovanni and Campanella. "How about you kids?
Won't you have some?"

Giovanni, somewhat provoked at being called a
kid, made no reply, but Campanella said, "Yes, thank
you."

Finally the lighthouse keeper had his hands
free, and he went and softly laid apples on the laps
of the sleeping children.

"Thank you very much," said the young man.
"Where are these marvelous apples grown?" he went
on, examining his apple intently.

"Of course there's farming around here, but in
general it's arranged that good things come up on
their own," answered the lighthouse keeper. "Agriculture isn't much bother. Normally, if you plant the

seed of your choice, it will come up by itself. Now our rice, for example, doesn't have husks like the rice in the Pacific area, and the grains are ten times bigger, and have a nice fragrance, too.

"Why, what you have where you come from isn't agriculture at all! There isn't even the least bit of an apple or a cake! Over there everything varies from farmer to farmer, and a nice scent blows off right away on the first breeze."

Suddenly the little boy blinked his eyes wide open. "Oh! I just had a dream about Mom! She was in a place with a fine bookcase and books, and she reached out her hand to me with a great big smile, and I said, 'Mom, shall I pick some apples and bring them to you?' and I woke up, and . . . here . . . this is that train."

"That's the apple in your lap," said the young man. "This nice old man gave it to you."

"Thank you! Hey, Kaoru is still sleeping. I'll wake her up. Sis! Look, you have an apple! Wake up and see!"

The little girl opened her eyes with a smile and then, as if bedazzled, pressed her hands to her eyes. Then she looked at the apple.

The boy was gobbling his apple as if it were pie. The lovely peeling he had removed fell spinning like a corkscrew, and before it touched the floor dissolved softly in a shimmering light. Giovanni and Campanella put the precious apples in their pockets.

The Mysterious Forest

ON THE BANK ACROSS THE RIVER AND DOWNSTREAM, they saw a dense green wood, on the branches of whose trees shone countless ripe olives. A tall, tall triangular sign stood in the midst of the trees, and out of that wood came a sound of inexpressible beauty, half bell, half xylophone, that floated melting, then sinking into the wind. The young man trembled with the thrill of it. And as they listened silently to the music, roundabout them the carpetlike expanse of the pale green grove opened out, and a pale mist, white as candlewax, seemed to flit across the face of the sun.

"Oh! Look at those crows!" cried Campanella's neighbor, the girl named Kaoru.

"Those are no crows. They're magpies!" Campanella said, as if scolding her, and Giovanni smiled at the little girl's embarrassment.

The black birds, flock on flock of them, formed a long line that reflected the pale light glinting from the river below.

"They're magpies all right—you can tell by the pointed tuft behind the head," interceded the young man.

Now the triangular sign in the middle of the woods came directly in front of the train, and from far behind they heard the familiar strains of Hymn 306. There seemed to be a great many singers. The young man's face suddenly paled. He stood up and seemed about to go back toward the music, but then he changed his mind and sat down again.

Kaoru pressed her handkerchief to her face,

and even Giovanni found himself sniffling. But then someone somewhere in the train picked up the song and, the volume rising steadily, Giovanni and Campanella also joined in. And the green grove of olive trees, shining brightly, gradually disappeared into the dim distance of the Milky Way. The marvelous instruments and their music faded into the echo of the train and the murmur of the wind.

"Peacocks! Look at the peacocks!"

"There were a lot of them," answered Kaoru. "I bet that forest is the constellation of the harp player. And all the players in all the orchestras of the past would be gathered there, too."

Over that forest, now grown tiny, like a single button of seashell, Giovanni could make out the reflection of light cast by the opening and closing of the peacocks' feathers.

"And that was the voice of the peacocks we heard before," Campanella explained to the girl.

"Yes. There must have been at least thirty of them," she answered. Giovanni didn't know whether to feel happy or sad. He wanted to say. "C'mon, let's get off here and walk around," but he felt tongue-tied. A strange object in the river had caught his eye, and his face twisted into a horrible frown.

Whatever it was, it was long, black, and slippery. Jumping up over the invisible water of the river, it arched rather like a bow, and again plunged into the water. As Giovanni looked more carefully, he saw, with amazement, the same sort of thing much closer by. And then here and there, and all over, those strange, slippery black things were bounding from the water, arching in midair and diving headfirst back into the river. They all seemed to be swimming, like fish, in an upstream direction.

"Oh—what are they? Look how many there are!" Kaoru called to her brother. "What can they be?"

"Yes, what are they, anyway?" The student also stood up.

"It's the strangest-looking fish I've ever seen," said Kaoru. But Campanella, who was also looking out the window, knew the answer. "They're dolphins."

"I've never seen a dolphin before," said Kaoru, "but don't they live in the ocean?"

"Dolphins are not confined to the sea." From somewhere far off that strange deep voice came again.

The really curious thing about the figures described by the dolphins was how they leaped from the water with their flippers lowered and motionless, and then, lowering their heads discreetly, plunged back into the water with their flippers in exactly the same position. Where they broke the surface, the invisible water was flecked with blue flamelike waves.

"Are dolphins a kind of fish?" Kaoru asked Campanella. Her little brother had sunk back in his seat exhausted and was again sound asleep.

"Dolphins aren't fish—they're mammals, like whales," answered Campanella.

"Have you ever seen a whale?"

"Yes, I have—and the only part of the whale you can see is the head and the black tail. When they spout, they look just like the pictures in books."

"Whales are huge, aren't they?"

"Whales are big, but the baby whales are about the same size as dolphins."

"That's right—it was in the Arabian Nights!" said Kaoru, toying with her slender silver ring.

Giovanni was becoming unbearably irritated, and he thought to himself—"Campanella, I'm getting out of here—I've never seen a whale or anything." But he bit down hard on his lip and looked out the window.

The dolphins were now out of sight, and the river was split in two by an island. In the center of that pitch black island a tall, tall tower had been erected, and at the top stood a man in a floppy coat wearing a red hat. With a red flag in one hand and a green flag in the other he was looking up into the sky and signaling. As Giovanni watched, the man waved the red flag vigorously, and then suddenly he put the

UNDER THE VAST, BEAUTIFUL, VIOLET SKY, TENS OF THOUSANDS
OF SMALL BIRDS WERE PASSING IN COUNTLESS FORMATIONS.

red flag down somewhere behind him and, holding the green flag as high as he could, waved it violently just like an orchestra conductor with a baton. And in no time, with a sound like pattering rain, cluster on cluster of black objects flew overhead, moving with the speed of bullets toward the other side of the Milky Way.

Giovanni thrust himself halfway out the window and looked up. Under the vast, beautiful, violet sky, tens of thousands of small birds were passing in countless formations, warbling as they went.

"The birds are migrating!" exclaimed Giovanni, his head out the window.

"Hurray!" Campanella also looked up at the sky.

Then the man standing on the tower abruptly raised the red flag and began to wave it wildly. Immediately the flocks of birds stopped in their course, and at the same time there was a dull thudding sound in the river valley. And then all lapsed into silence. Again the red-capped signalman raised the green flag and shouted (and they could hear his voice clearly), "Migratory birds cross now! Migratory birds now!" And once more the tens of thousands of birds moved in formation across the sky.

Kaoru, too, put her head out the middle window, between the boys, and looked up at the sky, her cheeks pretty and sparkling, "What a lot of birds—and how very pretty the sky is!" But Giovanni said nothing in reply and just stared vacantly up at the sky. Biting down hard on his lip, all he could think was what a nuisance and a bother girls were.

Kaoru heaved a little sigh and slunk off to her seat in silence. Campanella, as if to sympathize, pulled his head in, too, and looked at his map.

"Is he directing the birds?" Kaoru asked Campanella softly.

"He's signaling to the migratory birds—I think it's because they're firing off rockets somewhere," Campanella answered a little uncertainly. And the coach fell silent.

Giovanni wanted to pull his head back inside

the coach, but he really didn't feel like showing his face in that bright light just then, so he stayed where he was, whistling out the window, stifling the urge to speak.

"Why am I so sad?" he wondered. "I have to get hold of myself better than this. There are little blue smoky fires on that bank over there. It looks so cool and quiet. Maybe if I watch carefully I can be as calm as that." Giovanni stared out the window holding his hot, aching head glumly in both hands. "Oh," he thought, "isn't there anyone who'll stay with me all the way to the end? Campanella's having a great time talking to that girl, but me . . . I'm miserable."

From the New World

AS GIOVANNI'S EYES AGAIN FILLED WITH TEARS, THE Milky Way dissolved into an utterly distant misty whiteness.

Then the train climbed out of the riverbed to run along the top of the cliffs, and as it progressed down-stream the banks and cliffs on the other side seemed to be rising, too. Huge stalks of corn came into sight, their leaves curled round and round, and, under the leaves, beautiful green ears with reddish hairs, through which they caught a glimpse of pearl-like kernels.

The number of stalks steadily multiplied until they formed a line between the railbed and the edge of the cliff. Giovanni found himself pulling back from his window to look out the windows on the other side. There, as far as the horizon of that heavenly field, great corn stalks rose almost everywhere, swishing in the breeze, and the tips of their lovely curled leaves, flecked with dew, shone green and red, and flashed fire like diamonds catching the full light of midday.

"That's corn, isn't it?" Campanella said, but Giovanni, still down in the dumps, grunted, "I guess so" without turning his eyes from the field.

Now the train was slowing down, and after passing a number of signal lights and switches it came to a stop at a small station. The pale station clock showed exactly the second hour. The wind died to nothing and the train stood perfectly still as the tick-tock of the pendulum drifted out over the hushed and silent fields, sure and steady, marking out the time. Then, between the swings of the pendulum, they made out a faint, faint melody drifting like a thread from the furthermost limit of the fields.

"It's the New World Symphony," Kaoru said softly, looking up. But the tall young man in the black suit, along with nearly everyone else in the train, had drifted off into gentle dreams.

"What's wrong with me," wondered Giovanni, "that I don't feel any better in a nice peaceful place like this? Why am I so lonesome and all alone? But Campanella has really gone too far! He comes riding on the train with me, and then the only one he talks to is that little girl—I'm really miserable." Giovanni buried his face in his hands and stared out the window.

The train, with a blast of transparent sound from its glass whistle, began to roll smoothly along, and Campanella joined in with a dreary star-traveling whistle of his own.

"By jiminy, these are tough hills!" exclaimed an old man behind them.

"When you plant corn," he continued, "you've got to dig yourself a two-foot hole for the seed or it won't come up."

"It won't? . . . It must be quite a ways down to the river."

"I'd say about 2,000 to 6,000 feet. We're coming to a steep gorge now."

Giovanni found himself musing that this must be the Colorado Plateau. Kaoru, pressing her sleeping little brother close, had a faraway look in her black eyes—not from seeing something outside but from being lost in thought. Campanella whistled lonesomely to himself, and the sleeping face of the little boy looked like an apple wrapped in silk.

Suddenly the corn was gone, and a vast black plain opened out ahead of them. The New World Symphony flowed clearer and louder from over the horizon. And in the middle of the pitch black plain appeared a single Indian running at full tilt in pursuit of the train. He wore a headdress of white feathers and was fitting an arrow to his little bow.

"Indians! Look, Kaoru, it's an Indian!" cried Tadashi. The young man in the black suit came awake and both Giovanni and Campanella jumped to their feet.

"He's running this way—really running! He's chasing us!" said Kaoru.

"No—he's not chasing the train. He's either hunting—or dancing," said the young man in a far-away voice, as if he had forgotten where he was. He stood with his hands in his pockets.

Indeed, it half looked as if the Indian were dancing. In the first place, the way he was stepping was too wild to be taken seriously. Then he made a sudden sharp stop, his white headdress pitching forward as if about to fall off, and aimed his bow toward the sky. A single crane came wobbling down into the widespread arms of the Indian, who, after a fresh burst of running, was there waiting for it.

The Indian watched them, smiling happily with the crane in his arms as he swiftly dwindled to nothingness in the distance. There was a double flash from the insulators on the telephone poles, and then they were back in corn country again.

Looking back out the window on his side, Giovanni saw that the train was now running along the top of a high, high cliff. Far below, the river flowed on by, spreading out vast and bright.

"It's downhill from here on. It goes down to water level all at once, and that's no joke. Why, the slope is so steep the trains can't make it back up! Here goes! We're picking up speed already."

Faster and faster still the train went down, and, as the train skirted the edge of the cliff, the bright river could be glimpsed below.

Giovanni found his spirits steadily rising. When the train passed a dejected-looking child standing in front of a small shack, he called out, "Hi!" without a second thought.

The train kept on picking up speed. The passengers held on tight to their seats to avoid being pitched over backward. Giovanni and Campanella couldn't help laughing out loud—and now the heavenly river was right beside the train, throbbing with dazzling light as if it had been flowing swiftly through rapids. Pinks flowered here and there along the riverbank. At length the train slowed to a more leisurely pace.

On the cliffs on both sides they saw flags emblazoned with a star and pickax emblem.

Giovanni finally broke the silence. "I wonder what those flags stand for?"

"I don't know—and they're not on the map. There's an iron boat."

"Well . . ."

"Maybe there's a bridge under construction," suggested Kaoru.

"Hmm . . . they look like the flags of the Army Engineers. On a bridge-building exercise, maybe. But, there are no soldiers in sight."

Then, near the far bank and a bit downstream, there was a flash on the surface of the invisible galactic water, and a towering geyser erupted with a terrifying noise.

"They're blasting! They're blasting!" Campanella jumped for joy.

As the pillar of water drifted away, huge salmon and trout were pitched high in midair where, describing perfect circles, they turned—their bodies twinkling white and glistening—and fell back into the water.

Giovanni was in such a good mood now that he, too, felt like jumping for joy. "It's the Sky Engineers Battalion! How about that! Trout and salmon flying up out of the water! I've never been on a trip this much fun. Never!"

"If we were closer, we could see a lot of trout, I bet. There must be a lot of fish in that water!"

"Are there little fish, too?" Kaoru asked, drawn into the conversation.

"Sure there are! If there are big ones, there've got to be little ones, too. But we're too far off to make out the little ones."

"Oh! That must be the shrine of the Twin Stars!" Tadashi suddenly cried, pointing out the window.

Opposite them at the top of a low hill stood two small shrines that seemed to be constructed of crystal. "Mother used to tell me the story of the Twins. And there are their two little crystal shrines, side by side," said Kaoru.

"Tell the story! What's this about twins?"

"I know," said the boy. "The Twins went to play in a field and got in a fight with a crow."

"No, that's not it," said his sister. "It was on the banks of the heavenly river. Mother told me all about it."

"And along came a shooting star—woosh! woosh!"

"Tadashi! Behave yourself! That's not it at all— that's another story."

"And now they're over there playing the flute, aren't they? . . . They've gone out to sea."

"That's all wrong, silly! They came from the sea."

"Oh, yes, I know! I'll tell the story."

The Scorpion's Fire

THE OPPOSITE BANK OF THE RIVER SUDDENLY LIT up with red. The red peeped through the pitch black willow trees, and the invisible waves of the heavenly river, too, were flecked here and there with red, needlelike gleams. In fact, on the field across the river a great fire seemed to be burning, its towering black smoke rising as if to char even the cool violet heavens.

Raging drunkenly on, the flames were more beautiful than lithium and redder than rubies.

"What kind of fire is that? I wonder what they can be burning to get such red flames," said Giovanni.

"It's the Scorpion's fire," replied Campanella, again referring to his map.

"If it's the Scorpion's fire, I can tell you about it," said Kaoru.

"What's all this about the Scorpion's fire?" asked Giovanni.

"The scorpion burned to death. And the fire is still burning. My dad used to tell me the story."

"A scorpion is a kind of bug, isn't it?"

"Yes, it's a bug, but it's a good kind."

"It is not!" broke in Tadashi. "I saw a scorpion in alcohol at the museum. On its tail it had a spike like this, and if you get stung by that you die! That's what the teacher said."

"That's right, but it's still a good bug. This is what my father said: Long ago in a field in India there was a scorpion, and he lived by killing little insects and things and eating them. Then one day a weasel found the scorpion and was about to eat him up. The scorpion ran away as fast as he could, but finally the weasel seemed to have him cornered. All of a sudden, there was a well in front of him and the scorpion fell in. No matter how he struggled, he couldn't get back out, and he started to drown. So then the scorpion said: 'I have taken the lives of I don't know how many living things in my time. But when the weasel tried to catch me, how I tried with all my might to escape! In spite of that, I end up here. Why didn't I just quietly accept my fate and give myself up to the weasel? If I'd done that, the weasel would have had food to live one day longer. Oh, God, look into my heart! Instead of throwing my life away vainly like this, grant that my body may be used for the true welfare of all!'

"So he prayed, and the scorpion's body broke into beautiful crimson flames. He was placed in the heavens to light the darkness of the night. And my father said that fire will burn forever. So, really, that's what that fire is."

"That's what it is! Look, everyone—those signals are set exactly in the shape of a scorpion!" Giovanni saw that beyond the fire stood three triangular signs arranged like the legs of a scorpion; five other signs formed the tail and the sting.

Brightly, brightly without a sound the Scorpion's beautiful crimson fire burned, deep red, beautiful, and soundless. As the fire gradually passed out of sight behind them, they heard sounds of indescribable gaiety—musical instruments, and whistles, and the scent of flowers, and boisterous voices. It seemed as if they were coming to a town at festival time.

"Sagittarius, send down rain!" The little boy next to Giovanni (who had been sleeping again) shouted suddenly, looking out the opposite window.

Ahhh . . . there stood a great deep blue fir tree,

looking just like a Christmas tree, covered with tiny lights like a thousand fireflies at a convention.

"Tonight's the Milky Way Festival, isn't it?"

"And that's the Milky Way Village," Campanella promptly added.

The Southern Cross

"WE'LL BE ARRIVING AT THE SOUTHERN CROSS SOON—get ready to get off," the young man said to them.

"I'm staying on the train a little longer," responded Tadashi.

Kaoru stood up uneasily and began to get ready. But she seemed reluctant to part from Giovanni and Campanella.

"We've got to get off here," said the young man, looking down at Tadashi and pressing his lips together.

"I don't want to! I'm staying on the train and riding some more first."

Giovanni, unable to bear it, said, "Ride along with us! Our tickets are good for going on forever."

"But we really must get off now," said Kaoru sadly. "This is the place for going to Heaven."

"Who wants to go to Heaven? We have to make a place even better than Heaven right here. That's what my teacher said."

"But Mom is up there, and furthermore, God said so Himself."

"That kind of god is false!"

"Your god is false!"

"He is not!"

"What kind of god is your god?" The young man broke in, laughing.

"I'm not sure, really. But . . . anyway, He's the one true God," said Giovanni.

"Of course the true God is the only one."

"Anyway, my God is that one true God."

"Well, then, there you are! And I pray that

THEY COULD MAKE OUT ONLY THE RADIANT LEAVES
OF MANY WALNUT TREES STANDING IN THE MIST, AND
ELECTRIC SQUIRRELS WITH GOLD HALOS PEEPING OUT OF
THE MIST WITH MISCHIEVOUS FACES.

you'll be meeting us before the true God." The young man pressed his hands together gravely, and Kaoru, too, was praying.

At that precise moment, in the far distance of the Milky Way's downstream course, a cross, bejeweled with bright orange and blue lights, appeared, standing shimmering in the midst of the river. Its top was lost in a pale cloud, circular like a halo.

The inside of the train was thrown into commotion as all the passengers (just as they had before at the Northern Cross) stood up and began to pray. On all sides there were cries of joy—cries like those of children picking out gourds for the Milky Way Festival. As the cross gradually came parallel to their window, they saw that the silver cloud, pale like the twirling skin of an apple, was gently, ever so gently, revolving.

"Alleluia! Alleluia!" Brightly and happily the passengers' voices resounded together. From far off in the distant cold depths of the sky came the clear, bracing, indescribable blast of a trumpet.

The train gradually eased to a full stop directly opposite the cross in a blaze of signal lights and street lamps.

"Well, this is where we get off." The young man took Tadashi's hand, and Kaoru, adjusting her coat and straightening her collar, slowly followed them out of the train.

"I guess it's goodbye!" she said, looking back at Giovanni and Campanella.

"Goodbye!" said Giovanni—gruffly, but in fact he was only struggling to hold back his tears.

Kaoru looked back once more with big sad eyes, and then they were gone. The car, already only half full, abruptly emptied out and was left deserted with the wind blowing about it in gusts. Looking out, the boys could see the passengers lined up, kneeling on the bank of the Milky Way in front of the Cross. They saw a figure robed in solemn whiteness passing over the invisible water of the heavenly river, hand extended toward them.

But then the glass whistle sounded, and, just as the train began to move, a silver fog came flowing softly upstream and their view was blotted out. They could make out only the radiant leaves of many walnut trees standing in the mist, and electric squirrels with gold halos peeping out of the mist with mischievous faces.

Now, soundlessly, the fog rolled away once more. They saw a street, lined with little street lamps, that looked like a highway to somewhere. For some time it ran along beside the track, and as they passed the lights, the boys saw those tiny specks of red flame blink on and off, as if in greeting.

Looking back, they saw that the cross was now incredibly tiny and far away. It looked like something you could hang around your neck. They wondered about Kaoru and Tadashi and the young man. Were they still kneeling on the bank, or had they set out in whatever direction it is that leads to Heaven? But it was so blurry, they couldn't tell.

Giovanni heaved a deep sigh. "Campanella, it's just you and me again. Let's stick together all the way, whatever happens! . . . You know, if it's for everyone's happiness, I'm ready to have my body burned like that Scorpion—even a hundred times."

"Ummmm. I feel the same." Campanella's eyes were swimming with gentle tears.

"But—what is it that will make everyone happy?" continued Giovanni.

"I don't know," Campanella muttered.

"Anyway, we're going to hold on!" said Giovanni with an explosion of breath as if his chest were brimming with new-found energy.

"Ah—that's the Coal Sack. It's the hole in the sky!" Campanella seemed to shrink back as he pointed to a spot in the heavenly river. Giovanni, too, was shaken as he looked over there. Beyond on the heavenly river, a great black emptiness opened out.

However he strained his eyes, he couldn't tell how far down the bottom might be, or what might be inside—it only made his eyes smart. "I wouldn't be afraid in a big dark place like that anymore," he

"AH—THAT'S THE COAL SACK. IT'S THE HOLE IN THE SKY!"
. . . BEYOND ON THE HEAVENLY RIVER, A GREAT BLACK
EMPTINESS OPENED OUT.

said. "I'd go looking in there for what would make people happy. You and me—together to the end!"

"Together!" echoed Campanella. "Hey! Don't those fields look great, and everyone's gathered there, and—that must be Heaven itself! And there's my mother!" Campanella cried out, pointing suddenly out the window to a beautiful place he saw in the distance.

Giovanni looked where he was pointing, but all he could see was dim, white, rolling smoke, and nothing at all like what Campanella was describing. Feeling indescribably lonesome, Giovanni looked aimlessly around. He saw two telephone poles standing on the opposite bank, their arms linked as if joined in an embrace.

"Campanella, we'll stick together, right?" Giovanni turned as he spoke and ... in the seat where Campanella had been sitting until now, there was no Campanella, only the dark green velvet seat.

Giovanni burst into tears and everything went black.

The Professor

"WHAT ON EARTH ARE YOU CRYING FOR? LOOK THIS way a minute." From behind Giovanni came that gentle, cellolike voice he had heard so many times before. Giovanni turned around in amazement, wiping the tears from his eyes.

In the seat where Campanella had been before sat a pale, thin-faced man wearing a big black hat and holding a large book. He was smiling kindly.

"Your friend has gone a long way off, Giovanni.

Tonight he really went a long way, and it's no use looking for Campanella anymore."

"But—why? I said I was going to go straight on with Campanella!"

"Of course, everyone thinks that. But you can't go together. And everyone is Campanella. Everyone you meet, Giovanni—every time you ride on a train—everyone you ride with and eat apples with. So it's just as you were thinking before. Take every opportunity to look for the greatest happiness of all people, and quickly join them on their way. That's the only way, Giovanni, that you can go on forever with Campanella."

"That's just what I'll do! But how should I go about it?"

"Well, now . . . I'm working on the same thing myself. First, Giovanni, hold tight to your ticket when you go. Then you'll have to study hard. You must have learned some chemistry in school. You know that water is made up of oxygen and hydrogen.

Everyone accepts that without question now, because if you experiment, well, you can see that that's what it really is.

"But in the old days, some people said water was made of mercury and salt and others said it was made of mercury and sulphur, and there were all kinds of disputes about it. Just like every man, without exception, says that his god is the true God. But the things that people who believe in different gods do to each other are enough to make you shed tears. Then they dispute about whether our hearts are good or evil—an argument no one wins. But if you study hard so that by experiment you can divide true thoughts from false thoughts—if you can just figure out how to set up the experiment—why then, Giovanni, faith will become just like science.

"But, well, look at this book a minute. All right? This is a dictionary of history and geography. Now on this page you see the geography and history of 2200 B.C. written down.

"Take a good look! It isn't the way things really were in 2200 B.C. It's what people in 2200 B.C. thought of history and geography. So one page of this book stands for a whole volume of history and geography. All right? And the things written on this page are pretty much true. If you check it out, the evidence will pour in. But then you'll wonder where that gets us and, lo and behold, here's the next page."

"This is 1000 B.C. The geography and history have changed quite a bit, eh? This is how it was seen at that time. Don't frown like that! And we're the same way—our bodies, our ideas, the Milky Way, the railroad, history—all are the way we feel them.

"Look here! Take it easy, try to see things my way a little, all right?" And he raised a finger, and silently lowered it.

All at once Giovanni felt himself, and his thoughts, and the train, and that scholar, and the heavenly river, and everything coming together in a radiant flash. Then, silently, it was gone. Flash! It lit up and was again extinguished. And when everything lit up, the whole wide world opened out, and all history with it in that flash. Softly it died out into emptiness, and that was all. The flashes came at faster intervals—and then, very soon after, Giovanni found everything back just as it had been before.

"How's that? So you see, Giovanni, your experiment will have to include both the beginning and the end of this disjointed thought process. And that is a difficult thing. But, of course, it's all right if you limit yourself to the thought of a single time. . . ."

"Ah—look at that! Those are the Pleiades and, Giovanni, you'll have to unlock the chains of those stars!"

From beyond the black horizon a rocket of pale fire rose, bursting like daylight across the sky and flooding the coach with light. And the rocket, hanging high in the sky, continued to shine.

"Oh, it's the Magellanic Cloud! Well, one thing for sure—I'm going to look for the realest real happiness, for myself, and my mother, and Campanella, and everyone!" Giovanni bit his lips and looked longingly at that cloud of stars. If only everyone could find that highest happiness!

"Well, hold tight to your ticket. From now on, Giovanni, it will not be on the dream railroad, but in the heat and strife of the real world that you'll have to go pressing on with long strides. But whatever happens, keep that ticket, the only one of its kind, a real ticket from the Milky Way! Don't lose it!"

And, even with that cellolike voice still in his ears, the wind rose and the heavenly river slipped far off into the distance. Giovanni found himself back on his feet on the grassy hilltop. He heard the soft footsteps of the professor approaching from a great distance.

"Thank you! I've made a fine experiment! I'd been thinking I might try sending my thoughts from a distance to someone in a quiet spot like this. Everything you said is recorded in my notebook. If you act just as you resolved in your dream, all will be well. And from now on, come to my place when you need advice about anything. Anything!"

"I'll do just as I said. I'll look for true happiness," Giovanni said his voice ringing.

"Well, then—goodbye. Here's your ticket."

The professor put a tightly folded piece of green paper into Giovanni's pocket. And then he disappeared beyond the pole under mid-heaven.

Giovanni ran straight down the hill. Then he felt something heavy and clinking in his pocket. Stopping in the middle of the woods, he checked and found that the strange green ticket from his dream was wrapped around two big coins.

"Thank you, Professor! Mom, I'm going to get the milk right away!" cried Giovanni, breaking into a run. And a great many things gathering in his heart at once, Giovanni felt something both sad and new inside. Vega and the cluster of stars had traveled far to the west, and again, dreamlike, were extending their rays like legs to the earth.

The Bridge

GIOVANNI OPENED HIS EYES. HE HAD BEEN SLEEPING exhausted in the grass on the hilltop. His chest felt strange and feverish, and cold tears lined his cheeks. He leaped up and looked around. Just as before, the city below was lit with many lights, but somehow that light seemed brighter than before.

The Milky Way, where he himself had just been in a dream, was spread out the same as before, white and dimly visible in the distance. It seemed particularly smoky just above the deep black southern

FAR DOWNSTREAM, ON A SHOAL REACHING INTO THE
RIVER, A CROWD OF MEN STOOD SHARPLY OUTLINED
AGAINST THE DARKNESS.

horizon. To the right, the red stars of Scorpio twinkled exquisitely. It seemed, on the whole, that the
position of the stars hadn't changed much.

Giovanni ran breakneck down the hill, his
mind on his mother who was waiting and had not
had her supper yet. Swiftly he ran through the dark
pine woods and, turning in at the pale white fence
of the farm, went in through the same gate in the
front of the dark barn. Someone seemed to be there
now—there was a wagon that hadn't been there
before, loaded with two barrels of something.

"Anybody home?" called Giovanni.

"Yeah!" A man wearing floppy white trousers
came out at once and stood before him. "What can
I do for you?"

"The milk didn't come to our place today."

The man immediately went back inside and
came out with a bottle of milk which he handed
over to Giovanni. "I'm really sorry. Just after noon
today I absentmindedly left the gate between the
cows and the calves open, and the calves got in

and drank half the milk," he explained with a smile.

"They did? Well, thanks. I must be going."

"Right—sorry about that!"

"That's okay."

Giovanni went out the dairy gate, tenderly carrying the bottle of still warm milk in both hands. For a while the way was lined with trees, then he was on the main street, and soon he came to the crossroads and turned off to the right in the direction Campanella and the others had gone to sail lights down the river. There the framework of the bridge rose dimly in the night sky. In front of the shops at the crossroads, women were gathered in groups of seven or eight, looking out toward the bridge and talking about something in a dull murmur. Over on the bridge, he could see a great many lights.

For no particular reason, Giovanni felt a chill sweep over his heart. He called out to some people nearby, "Has anything happened?"

"A child fell in the water!" someone answered,

and all the people turned together to stare at Giovanni.

Giovanni took off in a daze toward the bridge. The top of the bridge was so crowded with people that he couldn't see the water. A policeman in a white uniform was there, too. As if flying from the foot of the bridge, Giovanni jumped down to the broad riverbank below. By the water's edge a host of lights were moving busily up and down. On the dark embankment on the other side, too, seven or eight lights were moving. In between, the river, faintly lapping, no longer dappled by the lights of the floating gourds, flowed gray and silent.

Far downstream, on a shoal reaching into the river, a crowd of men stood sharply outlined against the darkness. Giovanni went toward them, just as he saw Masaru, a boy who had been with Campanella before.

Masaru came running up to him. "Giovanni! Campanella fell into the river!"

"How? When?"

"Zanelli was standing in one of the boats. He was trying to push the gourds out where the current could catch them. And the boat started to rock and he fell in himself. Right away, Campanella jumped in after him, and he managed to push Zanelli over to the boat and Kato grabbed him. But by then Campanella was out of sight."

"Everybody must be looking for him!"

"Everyone came right away. Campanella's father came, too. But they haven't found him. Zanelli was taken home."

Giovanni went on to where the crowd was standing. In the middle of the students and townspeople stood Campanella's father, a tall man in a black suit. His pale chin jutting out sharply, he looked intently at the watch on his right wrist.

All eyes were turned toward the river, and no one uttered a word. Giovanni's legs were shaky and trembling. Acetylene lamps, the kind used for night fishing, were flickering restlessly back and forth, and he saw the flowing river throwing up tiny gleaming

HE SAW THE FLOWING RIVER THROWING UP TINY GLEAMING
WAVES. THE WATER DOWNSTREAM REFLECTED THE MILKY
WAY SO PRECISELY THAT THE SKY ITSELF SEEMED TO BE
FLOWING UNDER THE BRIDGE.

waves. The water downstream reflected the Milky Way so precisely that the sky itself seemed to be flowing under the bridge.

Giovanni couldn't help feeling it was no use. Campanella was out of sight on the far bounds of that Milky Way.

But it seemed like the others were all waiting to hear Campanella call out from the waves, "I really swam a long way!" or turn up standing on some undetected shoal, waiting for someone to come and get him.

At last Campanella's father said gravely, "It's no use now! He fell in forty-five minutes ago."

Without a moment's hesitation, Giovanni ran up to the professor. He meant to say, "I know where Campanella has gone—I was with him there," but his throat choked up and he couldn't say anything.

For a time the professor peered down at Giovanni, as if expecting him to say something first. Finally he said politely, "You're Giovanni, aren't you? Thank you for what you did this evening."

Giovanni, without saying anything, simply bowed his head.

"Is your father back yet?" the professor asked, pressing his watch tightly.

"No." Giovanni shook his head vaguely.

"How's that? I got a very cheerful note from him just the day before yesterday. Said he'd be getting in about today, but I guess the ship was held up. Giovanni, you come over with the others after school tomorrow, hear?"

And the professor again looked off intently downstream, where the Milky Way glimmered brightly in the water.

Giovanni, his heart overflowing with so many things, left the professor without a word. Clutching the milk bottle, he ran pell-mell from the river's edge into town to tell his mother the good news. His father was coming home!

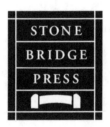

Stone Bridge Press books are sold online and at booksellers
around the world. Many are available as e-books.

For a complete list of Stone Bridge Press titles, download our catalog at
http://www.stonebridge.com/SBPCatalog.pdf

STONE BRIDGE PRESS, P.O. BOX 8208, BERKELEY, CA 94707
sbp@stonebridge.com / www.stonebridge.com

*Available to the book trade from Consortium Book Sales
and Distribution and major wholesalers*